The Confe$$ion$ and $ecret$ of Howard J. Fingerhut

The Confe$$ion$ and $ecret$ of Howard J. Fingerhut

by Esther Hershenhorn

illustrated by Ethan Long

Holiday House / New York

Library of Congress Cataloging-in-Publication Data
Hershenhorn, Esther.
The confe$$ion$ and $ecret$ of Howard J. Fingerhut /
by Esther Hershenhorn; illustrated by Ethan Long. — 1st ed.
p. cm.
Summary: Fourth grade entrepreneur Howard J. Fingerhut competes
with his classmates to win the H. Marion Muckley Junior Businessperson
of the Year Contest and writes a book about the experience.
ISBN 0-8234-1642-9 (hardcover)
[1. Business enterprises—Fiction. 2. Contests—Fiction.
3. Authors—Fiction. 4. Schools—Fiction.]
I. Long, Ethan, ill. II. Title.
PZ7.H432425 Co 2002
[Fic]—dc21   2001039304

To my long-ago friend.
Oh, the places we're going!
E. H.

Note to the Reader

I *might* change the names of some of the people, places, and things to protect the identities of the real people, places, and things. I'm not sure yet.

(Of course, I'll definitely change Spenser's name, but that's to protect *me*.)

Howard J. Fingerhut
Soon-to-be-announced winner of
the H. Marion Muckley Junior
Businessperson of the Year Contest

September 30

Contents

A Personal Message from Howard J. Fingerhut

Photo of author

(Probably my picture from Redbird Sports Camp, only minus the freckles.)

Hi! My name is Howard J. Fingerhut, but everyone calls me Howie. I am the author of the book you are reading.

Some authors of how-to books make all sorts of claims right here on this page. I won't do that, except to say that my book, *The Confe$$ion$ and $ecret$ of Howard J. Fingerhut,* will probably change your life. Also, my how-to book is not like any other. My how-to book has a diary in the middle.

The diary part will have my confe$$ion$. It will also keep track of my progress in the H. Marion Muckley Junior Businessperson of the Year Contest. That's a business contest that Muckley Milkshakes is sponsoring for my fourth-grade class at the Four Corners School in Mt. Olive, Missouri. I will write one chapter for each month instead of one page for each day. The first chapter is for September, and I am writing that today, September 30. The last chapter will be for June, and I will write that on June 15—the day I win the H. Marion Muckley Junior Businessperson of the Year Contest.

The how-to part will have my $ecret$. It will also include a lot of the important business stuff I learn at school.

This is what *you* will learn after you read my book:

  (1) how I started my lawn care
       business—A Boy for All Seasons;
  (2) how I kept my business running;
  (3) how I made a profit so big, I won
       the H. Marion Muckley Junior
       Businessperson of the Year Contest.

Book publishers, movie producers, and TV talk shows pay authors a lot of money for good books with confessions and how-to secrets. So while it was raining this morning, I looked through three of my parents' how-to books to see how they were written. They were:

How to Make History Come Alive for Your
    Students (My dad teaches history at
    Mt. Olive Consolidated High School);
How to Write Joke$ for Money (My mom
    writes schoolbooks, but she really wants to
    write jokes);
How to Teach an Only Child to Finish What He
    Starts (I don't have any brothers or sisters).

My mom said the Mt. Olive Public Library has a how-to book on how to write how-to books. I plan to check it out on the way home from soccer practice.

As you can see, I've written the attention-grabbing title, the Note to the Reader, and the Contents page, and I am almost finished writing the Personal Message. I plan to write very short chapters, except for Chapter One, which will have the contest details.

Oh, and I think I'll use subtitles the way how-to authors do. With subtitles, I can have *little* sections of information. This is very good for me, the author. I probably won't have a lot of writing time, between my sports career and lawn care business. This is also very good for you, the reader. No one likes to read chapters with long sections anyway.

Thank you,

Howie

P.S. Don't worry about the big words and fancy punctuation marks. I'm handing in this book for language arts extra credit.

Chapter One
September

How I Became Involved in This Contest in the *First Place* (Ha! Ha!)

I would never be writing this book if it weren't for my teacher, Ms. Robedeaux, and *Mrs.* H. Marion Muckley.

Oh, and Allyson Muckley, Mrs. Muckley's granddaughter.

Mr. H. Marion Muckley started Mt. Olive's world-famous drive-up ice-cream chain, Muckley Milkshakes. His milkshake machine is world famous, too. Mr. and Mrs. Muckley were married for a long time. When I was a baby, Mr. Muckley died very suddenly at a restaurant convention in Ohio. Mrs. Muckley misses him a lot.

Just so you know, from now on I'm calling the H. Marion Muckley Junior Businessperson of the Year Contest "The Contest."

For reasons you *don't* need to know, I will not mention Allyson's name ever again.

On the first day of school, even before we'd learned how to pronounce our teacher's name (Mizz *Row*-ba-doe), the person I'm not mentioning handed Ms. Robedeaux a Mt. Olive Chamber of Commerce New Neighbor gift basket.

Of course, guess whose grandmother is the Chamber of Commerce president?

Then guess who removed the basket's Magic Muckley *MOOLA*, handed it to her teacher, and invited her for dessert at Muckley's by the Mall?

"Guess what, boys and girls?" Ms. Robedeaux asked us the second day of school, even before she'd had the chance to send Spenser Baggey to the principal's office. "I found the perfect theme for our year of learning!"

She smiled at you-know-who. You-know-who smiled back.

My best friend, Nathan Lindeman, raised his hand. Like always, Nathan asked the question everyone was thinking.

"What do you mean by *theme,* Ms. Robedeaux?"

"Yeah," yelled Spenser. "What do you mean by *theme?*"

Ms. Robedeaux gave a very long answer (Ms. Robedeaux graduated from college last month and she has something called a Philosophy of Education), but here's the short version:

"Boys and girls," she explained, "children can learn so much more if all of their school subjects—math, reading, language arts, social studies, science, everything!—have something in common. A thread," she said. "A theme," she added.

Nathan raised his hand again. "For instance, Ms. Robedeaux?"

"Yeah," yelled Spenser. "How about a 'for instance'?"

My teacher winked at you-know-who. You-know-who winked back.

"How to run a business," Ms. Robedeaux said.

Here's the *Deal* on
Mrs. Muckley's Contest

This is my second subtitle joke. My mom says a sense of humor is very good for business. (Ha! Ha!)

But Mrs. Muckley said sort of the same thing when she finished speaking to us during math two weeks ago.

"For goodness' shakes!" she said when she first walked into our classroom. Her eyes were teary, and she sniffed and blew her nose a lot. "If only my H. Marion were here to see this."

You-know-who had hung Mr. Muckley's portrait front and center, right above our fire drill instructions. Chains of paper money—which Paige Alexander spent all night making—covered the ceiling in funny loops. Monica Santucci had decorated the back bulletin board with red hearts and Muckley Milkshakes menus. (The Muckley Milkshakes menus were really Paige's idea.) And everyone, including Spenser, wore a Muckley Milkshakes cow hat.

There was a lot of thanking. Mrs. Theodore, the principal, thanked Mrs. Muckley for sponsoring The Contest. Ms. Robedeaux thanked Mrs. Muckley for everything she'd be teaching us. And all three thanked you-know-who for bringing them together.

Then everybody posed for the contest kickoff picture. I'll tell my publisher to print it right here, in case you didn't see it in last Thursday's *Mt. Olive Gazette* (page 3). Unfortunately, the photographer was the one from last year's third-grade Field Day.

Of course, Elliott Throop asked the first contest question. In the kickoff picture, he's the very busy person at the end of the second row, punching in numbers on his tiny calculator.

"Ma'am," he said, "my grandfather and father talked about Muckley Milkshakes all the time, even before The Contest. I'm sure you know them. They own the Throop Bank of Missouri." Then he handed her his business card! "I'm Elliott Throop the Third.

"I was wondering," he asked, "if you checked the contest's numbers? You're giving each of us fifty dollars to start a contest business and there are twenty in the class. That's one thousand dollars."

Nathan corrected Elliott. In the kickoff

picture, Nathan's the one on my right, and he never needs a calculator, that's how smart *he* is. He's also a little pale and can't eat candy, but that's because of health reasons I have no business mentioning in a best-selling how-to book.

"Well, actually," Nathan said, "with the First Place Prize of one year's worth of any Muckley Milkshakes dessert, plus the two first-row seats to the Shriners circus next July, plus the silver milkshake-cup trophy, Muckley Milkshakes will be spending even more money."

Mrs. Muckley smiled, especially at Elliott. "As my H. Marion used to tell me, 'You worry about *your* numbers, dear. I'll worry about *mine.*'"

"My name's Howard," I told Mrs. Muckley when she finally called on me. "Howard J. Fingerhut, but everyone calls me Howie."

"Oh, for goodness' shakes!" she said. "I've heard so much about you! Didn't we meet at the third-grade Field Day?"

"I don't remember. Now here's my question," I said. "Are there any contest rules about what kind of business we can start?"

"Why, yes, Howie, there are. What a wonderful question. You're every bit as smart as I heard you were."

According to Mrs. Muckley's rules, we could start a business that makes something and sells it, let's say like a popcorn ball or a tie-dyed T-shirt.

"The something is called a *product*," Ms. Robedeaux said.

Or we could start a business that does a job for someone, let's say like baby-sitting pets or washing windows.

"The something's called a *service* then," Ms. Robedeaux explained.

It was at that exact moment that I looked out the window and saw three yellow oak leaves fall to the ground.

Last year Mt. Olive was named the Tree City of Missouri!

And the year before that, we had three winter blizzards!

And the year before that, we were on the cover of *Lawn and Gardens*!

"Lawn care!" I said, only louder than I'd meant to.

"What a wonderful contest business!" Mrs.

Muckley said. "My husband's first business as a boy was cutting grass!"

Spenser disagreed with Mrs. Muckley's opinion. In the kickoff picture, Spenser's the big kid who *should have been* in the back row except Mrs. Theodore made him stand next to *her.*

"You're too skinny, Fingerhut, to make money mowing lawns." He flexed his right arm. "Lawn care takes muscles."

You-know-who suggested I show Spenser my muscles. Instead I rubbed my biceps and listened to Mrs. Muckley.

"What an interesting question, Elliott," Mrs. Muckley was saying. "And, yes, this *is* a new and different business world since my husband invented his steel-blade milkshake pulsator. I can't imagine what H. Marion would think about dot-coms and e-mail and musical phones. All these tiny, tiny computer chips doing who knows what. My, my. For goodness' shakes!

"Of course, some things never change," Mrs. Muckley said. "Mr. Muckley believed in knowing each customer personally."

"Yeah," said Spenser. "Up close and personal!"

"Excuse me, Mrs. Muckley," I said. "You mean face-to-face, right?" I looked at Spenser. "Not *in* your face?"

Everybody laughed, except for Spenser.

And that's when Mrs. Muckley *sort of* agreed with my mom.

"My H. Marion enjoyed a good joke, too," she said.

The Inside *Scoop* on My Competition

This will be my last subtitle joke. I couldn't resist since I happened to be eating a Muckley's Waffle-cone Surprise. I'm also waiting for the rain to let up.

Amber Kirts thinks she knows everything. (In the kickoff picture she's the one with the biggest mouth telling everyone around her that I asked you-know-who to stand next to me.) No matter what Amber said in language arts yesterday, I have a very good chance of winning this contest.

I certainly have a better chance than *she* does. She started a fortune-telling business— Future, Inc.!

I definitely have a better chance than

you-know-who. *She* started a plant business—Muckley Greens and Seeds.

And Elliott and Spenser have no chance at all. Neither of them has started a business yet.

Amber made her comments after I read my name poem out loud. Ms. Robedeaux hung it up on the fourth-grade hall bulletin board but I know it by heart.

HOWIE
Hopeful
Original
Willing
Intelligent
Enthusiastic

My dad suggested another *H* word when I told my parents about this book and my contest business.

"*History* isn't a describing word," I explained to my dad.

"In your case it is, Howie," my dad explained to me. "You have a *history* that describes you to a T."

"Dad's right," my mom said. "Your adjectives are perfect, Howie, *except* when it comes to your money-making ideas. You enthuse too early and too much and too long, and you always count your chickens before they hatch. How about *hasty* and *excessive?*"

Dad agreed and threw in *worrisome.*

"Remember the seven stitches Mom needed when you asked her to baby-sit the Kupfermans' Chihuahuas?"

"Or what about Dad's broken toes when he held the ladder while you washed the Kupfermans' windows?"

They both reminded me of my soggy popcorn balls and the tie-dye paint that gave Grandma Millie's Senior Citizen Club a rash.

"History," my dad said, "is our greatest teacher."

"Well," I assured them, "this time is different."

My dad bit his lower lip. My mom chewed the skin on her right thumb's knuckle.

"You happen to be looking at the *new* Howie Fingerhut," I told them. I smiled my best smile. "New and Improved."

My dad bit his upper lip. My mom switched thumb knuckles.

"Really," I said. "I still have my freckles but other than that, Redbird Sports Camp changed my life."

Also, I explained, thanks to Mrs. Muckley, this time I had a business plan. I would rake, shovel, mulch, and mow, depending on the season.

"And the old-fashioned way, just like Mr. Muckley. No noisy leaf blowers or power mowers for me!"

My fall rate for raking was ten dollars per lawn.

I'd already signed up eight customers on Elm, Oak, and Maple, including Nathan's mom, and four of Grandma Millie's neighbors on Thornwood. Oh, and Dad's new principal, Mr. Busghetti (*Mis*-ter Bus-*get*-tee).

"Now, there's a lawn!" I said. "I'm charging him double."

With Mrs. Muckley's start-up money, I'd bought a three-month supply of orange plastic jack-o'-lantern leaf bags at Alexander Hardware, for that extra-special touch, and a used rake, salter, and mower at Grandma Millie's Senior Citizen Club's garage sale. Oh, and I had my business name—A Boy for All Seasons.

"Here," I said, and I showed them my book dedication.

To my parents, Warren and Judy Fingerhut, for always believing in me.

"It was supposed to be a surprise," I told them.

My mom bit her lip. My dad chewed on his thumb knuckle.

What You Will Find in the Next Chapter

Most authors of how-to books end their chapters with this subtitle, but I can't. How could I know on September 30 exactly what I'll write on October 31?

(Unless, of course, I hire Future, Inc. Ha! Ha!)

Anyway, what I do know is that during math on Wednesday, everybody with a contest business reported on his or her progress and how much money he or she earned. Then

Ms. Robedeaux taught us how to record that information on a bar graph.

Right now I'll ask my publisher to print Monica's bar graph, since Monica's an artist and has a special computer program that makes fancy letters.

All you'll need to do is look up my name— or Nathan's or Paige's—then follow the bar to read how much money we've earned.

Which now reminds me of something you *could* find in Chapter Two. In Chapter Two I will probably explain why Nathan's business, Schools R Us, jumped off to such an early lead.

Ms. Robedeaux's Class—Grade 4
Four Corners School

	$25	$50	$75	$100	$150
Paige Alexander—Ads by Alexander (advertising agency)				██████████	
* Spenser Baggey—Guardian Angel, Inc. (protection service)	███████				
Brendan Berks—Brendan's Snacks-a-Go-Go (fast food pickup and delivery)	███				
Jed and Ned Chen—Scrub-a-Dub (bike and car wash)	███				
Dominic Di Poppo—trade'em.com (sports cards)	███				
Howie Fingerhut—A Boy for All Seasons (lawn care)	███				
Haley Hoffstattler—Imindem.com (baby-sitting)	███				
Anthony Kalicki, Jr.—WheelzRUs (skateboarding lessons)	██████				
Jasmine Kim—SweetiePieSweets (cookies, cakes, and candies)	██████				
Amber Kirts—Future, Inc. (fortunes, palm reading)	███				
Nathan Lindeman—Schools R Us (school-related services)				██████████	
Mike McQuire—Mike-Moments Instant Photos (instant photos)	██████				
Allyson Muckley—Muckley Greens and Seeds (plants and seeds)	████				
Crissy Mull—Cards by Crissy (greeting cards)	███				
Luis Perez—BowWowWalk&Wash (dog walking and washing)	███				
Olivia Randall-Rogers—Say It with Feeling (letter-writing service)	███				
Monica Santucci—Art with a Heart (art services)	███				
Julianna Schlossberg—Jewels&Gems by Schlossberg (beaded jewelry and hair decorations)	████				
* Elliott Throop III—Mi$terBuck$ (money lending)	██				

* not listed on September bar chart

Chapter Two
October

I'm very glad I decided to use subtitles and write *little* sections of information. October has been a busy month.

My Mt. Olive Park District soccer team, the Supremes, won three of its last four games. (I kicked the winning goal in two of those games.) We *could* earn a play-off spot *if* we win next week.

I'm writing this chapter one day early. Here are three $ecret$ to help you run your business. I wanted to share four $ecret$, but my school's Trick-or-Treat Monster Bash starts at 6 P.M. sharp.

Howard J. Fingerhut's $ecret #1: It Pays to Advertise

Lucky for me that Paige Alexander started an advertising agency for her contest business—Ads by Alexander. (Did I mention that in the kickoff picture, Paige is the one with the long blond hair and dark blue eyes, holding the contest sign?)

Actually, Paige's business was a lucky thing for a lot of us. She said so herself when she invited me to her house three Fridays ago after school.

"Advertising, Howie, can make or break a business."

Paige and I were alone (!), except for her little brother P. J., who was upstairs with the chicken pox. She showed me the advertising slogans she'd written for her customers. She had them in an album she held on her lap.

"'Sow and grow with Muckley Greens and Seeds!' Catchy, don't you think, Howie?"

"Yes," I said.

"'The future is now with Future, Inc.!' Catchy, don't you think, Howie?"

"Yes," I said.

"You know, I also nicknamed Nathan 'Dr. Homework.'"

"Dr. Homework?"

"For his Schools R Us business. Nathan said I had a way with words."

"Of course," I said. "Dr. Homework."

Paige put down the album. Then she whispered in my ear, "A Boy for All Seasons leaves no leaf unturned!"

Fortunately, Paige had a wonderful one-time-only October special for first-time clients like me. One catchy slogan, one catchy ad, fifty flyers (on the colored paper of my choice), fifty business cards, and a Halloween tie-in promotion, all for the low price of $14.95.

"In cash," Paige said. "And you have to pay me now. And you have to agree to use Monica's design service."

She handed me Monica's business card: Art with a Heart.

Oh, and the $14.95 wouldn't cover a Web site.

"That's extra," Paige said, "but Nathan said it's worth it."

Paige flipped her hair back, then pushed it behind her ears.

"You know, Howie, since we have a business relationship now, why don't I just drop off some of your flyers at my dad's store, Alexander Hardware? They're having their Fall Bushel of Savings Sale. In fact, Mt. Olive Village leaf bags are only twenty-five cents each this week."

I wet down the hair part I've been training since camp.

"Well, I bought the orange plastic jack-o'-lantern bags, for that extra-special touch."

"Oh?" said Paige. "They're not just for decoration? You can fill them with leaves and the Village will pick them up?"

I paid Paige the money and asked for a receipt.

"You probably don't know this," I said, "but I'm writing a book, *The Confe$$ion$ and $ecret$ of Howard J. Fingerhut.* The *S*'s are dollar signs. Catchy, huh?"

"Sort of," said Paige. "And Amber already told me."

Paige handed me a five-dollar coupon for Ads by Alexander.

"Do you think you'll have space in your book, Howie, to mention my advertising agency?"

Her hair had fallen loose so she flipped it back again.

"I think so," I said. And it turns out I was right.

This is the *perfect* place to have my publisher print my business card.

My $14.95 paid off four times because that's how many new customers I signed up from my flyers! I look forward to meeting them when I rake their leaves.

Oh, and I signed up Mr. Montgomery, the Park District referee, but just for snow removal since he already had a leaf blower.

Howard J. Fingerhut's $ecret #2: The Customer Is Always Right

I have fifteen customers (including my parents and Grandma Millie) and fourteen have been very understanding about my soccer schedule. My customers on Thornwood have little lawns with maybe two trees, one in the front and one in the back. And Grandma Millie was a big help. (She said loading the wheelbarrow with leaves and pushing it around reminded her of the times she'd helped Grandpa before he died.) All of my customers had their own Mt. Olive Village leaf bags left over from the summer. Except for Grandma Millie and her next-door neighbors, the Kupfermans.

Nathan's mom *wasn't* understanding.

Last Monday before dinner I'd stopped by Nathan's. I had a 5 P.M. Schools R Us appointment. (Good old Dr. Homework was backed up for a week with everyone wanting to take his Junior Businessperson IQ Test. He squeezed me in, though, since I *am* his best friend.)

Anyway, Mrs. Lindeman saw my rake and thought I'd come to clean the yard. So I held up my shovel, my hoe, and my hose.

"I'm a Boy for All Seasons! Get it?" I asked.

"No," said Mrs. Lindeman.

I was very surprised. After all, she *is* Nathan's mom *and* she works at the library.

So I unbuckled my slicker.

"See?" I said. I wiggled both legs. "This year's soccer shin guards?" Then I snapped the waistband on my navy blue trunks. "Last year's basketball shorts?" I knuckle-tapped my hat. "My baseball helmet?" I crunched leaves with my right foot. "My dad's old golf shoes? It's my Halloween costume!" I explained, rebuckling my slicker. "Fall, winter, spring, summer? Rake, shovel, hoe, hose? I'm a boy for all seasons. Paige thought it up."

I handed Mrs. Lindeman my business card.

"Get it?" I asked. "'Leave? Leaf?'"

I'm pretty sure this time Mrs. Lindeman got it, but because she's a librarian, she talks very softly. I moved in close, the way people do with librarians. So close, in fact, I was reading her lips.

"How-ie!" she said. Her lips moved really slowly. "You have left *ev-er-y* leaf unturned since I hired you in Sep-tem-ber! There are squirrels, How-ie, from all over Missouri, lying three and four deep beneath this sea of dead maple leaves. The squirrels suff-o-ca-ted, How-ie, burying chestnuts for the winter."

Mrs. Lindeman removed my rake and held it in her hands.

"*Rake* is an action word, How-ie! When people rake, they sweep up leaves and put them in bags that they set on the curb for the Village to pick up. People do that in the fall, How-ie, and this is what it looks like." She raked a circle around me. "Get it?" she asked.

"I got it," I said.

"Repeat after me, How-ie."

I repeated after Mrs. Lindeman. "The cus-tom-er is al-ways right!"

I raked a circle around Nathan's mom. Then I raked the stone path. Then I raked the front stoop. I raked the front lawn and was raking the side path when I "bumped" into Spenser. At least that's what Spenser claimed.

"Watch it!" I said.

"Did you hear that, Dr. Homework?" Spenser yelled to Nathan. "Fingerhut said, 'Watch it!'"

Spenser, it turns out, was Nathan's 4:30 appointment. Spenser had needed some help with the contest business he'd started—Guardian Angel, Inc., a protection service! He also needed help with his long division.

Spenser handed me his business card. I recognized the hearts.

"It says 'Watch it!'" Spenser said.

"I can read," I told him.

"Pretty catchy slogan, huh? Paige thought it up."

Once Spenser left, Mrs. Lindeman turned on the back patio lights so I could finish raking. In the really dark areas, Nathan held two flashlights for me.

"I forgot to tell your mom what Vince Jerome, the WMTO weatherman, said last night. How leaf falling's been so unpredictable this season because it didn't rain in August, and September was so warm."

"You heard my mom, Howie."

"Right," I said. "And actually fall doesn't end for seven weeks."

"You heard my mom, Howie."

"Right," I said.

Mrs. Lindeman turned down my offer to spell "BOO!" on the front lawn with the jack-o'-lantern bags filled with leaves.

"Just put them on the curb by the driveway, Howie. There's a pickup tomorrow."

"Right," I said. "Oh, and no extra charge, Mrs. Lindeman, for bagging those dead squirrels. Which reminds me of something . . ."

"Bill me, Howie."

She shut the door.

"Right," I said.

I couldn't resist that personal touch, so I piled up the leaf bags into a giant pumpkin.

Howard J. Fingerhut's $ecret #3: You Can't Fight City Hall

Not *all* towns would consider a sculpture made from plastic leaf bags a "public obstruction," even if it *is* on public property, like the Lindemans' sidewalk. And I still say Mrs. Lindeman's next-door neighbor should have at least *heard* the street-cleaning truck coming before he backed his Jeep out of his driveway.

The brushes on those trucks make a lot of noise.

I told Mrs. Lindeman that because the pumpkin sculpture was *so* large, not all of the pumpkin was actually on the Lindemans' sidewalk. *Parts* of the pumpkin were on the Lindemans' front lawn.

"Maybe you won't have to pay the entire twenty-five dollars," I said.

"You mean *you* won't have to." She handed me the ticket.

"Oh," I said. "Right," I added.

Some towns and villages—like Mt. Olive, it turns out—are also very particular about residents using only specially approved bags for leaves and garden materials.

Mrs. Lindeman gave me her other ticket for fifteen dollars.

Oh, and so did the Kupfermans and Grandma Millie.

My family and I studied the fine print on all three citations.

"Village Ordinance L-two sixteen doesn't mention the words *plastic, dyed, or decorated*—" I said.

"Forget it," said my mom.

"It's history," said my dad.

Grandma Millie said, "You can't fight City Hall."

"But it says right here Mt. Olive is a *village*."

"You get the point, son."

"Right," I told my dad.

What You Won't Ever Find in Any Book of Mine

Because Monica now insists I pay her this publishing thing called a royalty, I've decided *not* to end each chapter with Monica's bar graph.

Instead I'll end with a joke and leave you laughing.

Spenser's coming to the Monster Bash dressed as an angel!

Make that two jokes.

Elliott's dressing up as that little Monopoly man with the top hat, cane, and short black jacket. He started his business—Mi$terBuck$. Amber said that Monica said that Paige thought up the dollar signs!

Chapter Three
November

Without going into a lot of detail, I'm writing this in the Learning Center because my class is putting on the fourth-grade Thanksgiving play tomorrow. It is a "dramatic presentation" of the favorite foods served in a Thanksgiving dinner. Ms. Robedeaux assigned us our parts. Then each of us had to write twelve lines that rhymed. Spenser and I are mixed vegetables. I'm the peas. He's the carrots. I am not complaining, since you-know-who is corn. We're waiting for a dress rehearsal with the rest of our dinner course—the turkey, squash, gravy, cranberries, and potatoes.

For this chapter, I'll ask my publisher to print my language arts assignment, "On the Job with Howard J. Fingerhut." It's an hour-by-hour report of my November 15 raking job *plus* the Mike-Moments Instant Photos I hired Mike McQuire to take. (Mike says that once I pay him, I can use the photos any way I want to.) Think of my report as a picture album that shows you how I run my lawn care business.

Mike also photographed Spenser—for free!—protecting shy people on the school bus, in the cafeteria, and on the playground during morning and afternoon recess.

Spenser suggested my publisher print *his* "On the Job" report, too, after he knuckle-knocked my head and recited these lines.

Peas and carrots go together
Every Thanksgiving, in good
   or bad weather.
Sister, brother, father, mother,
You can't have one without the other.

"Right, Fingerhut?"
"Wrong," I said.

On the Job with Howard J. Fingerhut

Date: Saturday, November 15
Customer: The Busghettis
Address: 2121 Oak
Service: leaf raking

9:00 A.M. Mike and I arrive at the Busghettis'. Notice I
do not have Village leaf bags because Mrs.
Busghetti told me on the phone she had a
"healthy supply." Also notice that the three
garage doors are *closed*.

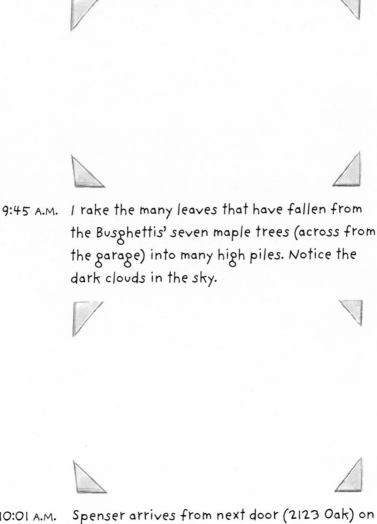

9:45 A.M. I rake the many leaves that have fallen from the Busghettis' seven maple trees (across from the garage) into many high piles. Notice the dark clouds in the sky.

10:01 A.M. Spenser arrives from next door (2123 Oak) on his dirt bike.

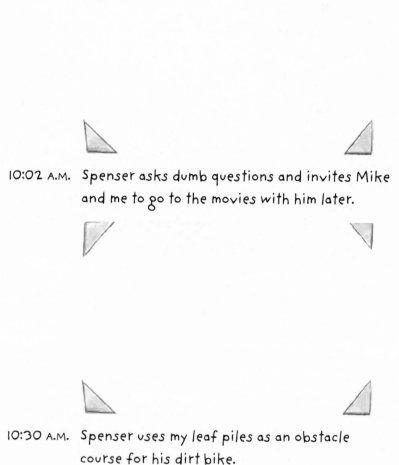

10:02 A.M. Spenser asks dumb questions and invites Mike and me to go to the movies with him later.

10:30 A.M. Spenser uses my leaf piles as an obstacle course for his dirt bike.

10:31 A.M.   Spenser continues to use my leaf piles as an
            obstacle course for his dirt bike.

10:32 A.M.   Mrs. Busghetti yells at Mr. Busghetti, "You're a
            penny-pinching cheapskate!" Mr. Busghetti
            yells back, "Well I happen to disagree."

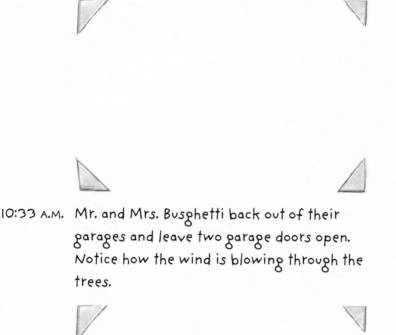

10:33 A.M. Mr. and Mrs. Busghetti back out of their garages and leave two garage doors open. Notice how the wind is blowing through the trees.

10:34 A.M. I look for Mrs. Busghetti's "healthy supply" of Village leaf bags in the third garage. There are no bags.

10:35 A.M. I bike around the corner to my home on Maple for my *Village* leaf bags.

10:36 A.M. Spenser attempts to jump my fifteen leaf piles with his dirt bike!

10:45 A.M.   It starts to rain. Notice the lightning in the sky and how the wind is blowing.

2:00 P.M.   The rain stops. My mom and I apologize to Mr. and Mrs. Busghetti for the leaf-raking disaster. Notice Spenser laughing in the driveway.

2:06 P.M.   My mom and I rake up the leaves that have blown *inside* the Busghettis' three garages.

4:05 P.M.   My mom and I bring seventeen filled Village leaf bags to the Busghettis' curb. Notice not one leaf bag "obstructs the view" or is on public property.

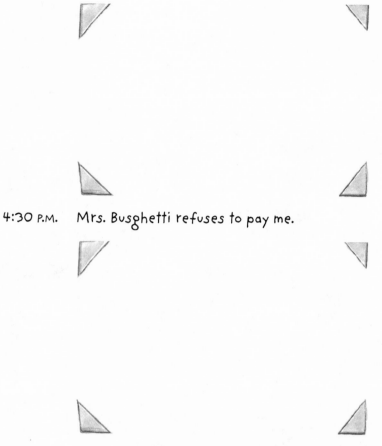

4:30 P.M.   Mrs. Busghetti refuses to pay me.

4:31 P.M.   I knock on Spenser's door and tell him he's not
             getting away with this. Oh, and that my mom
             says I'm crazy if I think I'm going to the movies.

Howard J. Fingerhut's Confe$$ion #1

In case you forgot, my confe$$ion$ will keep track of my contest progress.

Here's the formula Mrs. Muckley taught us so we could figure out how much money we are making.

INCOME ($$$ you collect)
− EXPENSES ($$$ you spend)
──────────────────────────
PROFIT

Some people, like Elliott, had very big *expense* numbers. He spent all fifty dollars of his contest start-up money on a Throop Bank loan to borrow even more money to lend to his customers.

Some people, like Paige and Nathan, had very big *income* numbers. Everyone hired them for advice and advertising.

Some people, like me, had two big numbers.

Oh, and a *slight* collection problem I'll turn around next month.

Mrs. Muckley used my lawn care business for her blackboard example.

$170.00 (A Boy for All Season's fall income)
− $139.44 (A Boy for All Season's fall expenses)
$30.56 (A Boy for All Season's fall profit)

Mrs. Muckley told me not to worry. "Our Muckley's off the Square is having trouble, too, Howie. Besides," she said, "there are all kinds of profits. Just think of the joy you're bringing to your customers."

Elliott handed me his business card. "Call me, Howie, when you run out of money."

"I won't," I said. "Call," I added. "Or run out of money. I have a *slight* collection problem. My customers owe me $110.00. And do me a favor, Elliott. Call me Howard."

"Yeah, well, here, Howard," Spenser said. He tossed me his business card. "Collection problems are right up my alley."

"Thanks, but no thanks. My customers will pay me."

Amber shook her head. "It's not in the stars, Howie. If I were you, I'd forget about your book . . . or," she said, "rewrite your name poem. Try *idiotic* and *embarrassing* for your *I* and *E*."

"If I were you," I said, "I'd predict Howard J. Fingerhut wins this contest! I'm a lucky Sagittarian. My grandma Millie said so. Plus, Vince Jerome predicted the snowiest winter ever." I handed her Vince Jerome's Winter Weather Forecast from the *Mt. Olive Gazette,* which I'll tell my publisher to print here along with my horoscope.

"The sun is in my sign. There'll be snow on the ground. I have three seasons left," I said, "to win The Contest!"

Forecast for December

Sagittarius (Nov. 21 to Dec. 20)

The sun is in your sign now, bringing you good luck. The prize is almost in your hand. What seemed like an obstacle will turn in your favor. White will be an important color.

Winter Weather Forecast

Meteorologist Vince Jerome, from WMTO, predicts an unusually snowy winter with unseasonably cold temperatures for most of Missouri.

Oh, and just in case you're interested:

MT. OLIVE PARK DISTRICT
SOCCER FINALS

Wolf League

Supremes **5, Dynamites 0**

(goals: Supremes—Fingerhut 3, Di Poppo 2)

Chapter Four
December

If Amber Kirts *really* wants to predict the future, I suggest she hire Vince Jerome. Winter's only one week old and already this month it's snowed twenty-nine inches! Vince says it's the snowiest December since 1959, the year Mr. Muckley opened his first Muckley Milkshakes. It snowed four to five inches every three to four days, including on my birthday. I'm piling up the profits *and* I'm getting a good workout. My basketball team—the Buccaneers—has an excellent chance of winning this year's Christmas vacation Mt. Olive Park District Holiday Tournament.

Vince said tonight on the six o'clock news that an Arctic Clipper is on the way. We'll have even more snow right through New Year's.

Oh, and temperatures are supposed to drop way below zero.

Now here are three more $ecret$ to help you run your business.

Howard J. Fingerhut's $ecret #4: Listen to Your Friends

In case you forgot, I'm a lucky Sagittarian. The first December snow came on a Saturday morning, right after my basketball practice. It was a light, fluffy snow, and my Big Foot shovel's specially designed blade made scooping and tossing easy. The houses on Thornwood have short driveways, so it took me only about one hour each to shovel them. Two of my customers on Oak phoned to say they'd moved. Mrs. Busghetti yelled through the mail slot that they'd just bought a snowblower. And the Moxleys on Elm said their son was home from college. By dinnertime Sunday, I'd shoveled each and every customer.

It was Mrs. Lindeman who suggested I needed some help. It was the day of the second snow and the Mt. Olive Chamber of Commerce's Downtown Winter Wonderland Night. Mrs. Muckley had arranged for my class to sell and advertise our services and products along with the rest of the town's businesses that night. My mom stayed in the car while I ran to the door to pick up Nathan.

"Howie!" Mrs. Lindeman said when she opened the front door. She definitely wasn't using her librarian's voice. "If you're not here to shovel my driveway, then turn around and get somebody who is!"

I measured the snow with my Schools R Us ruler. It was an early holiday present from Schools R Us.

"It's only two inches . . . and the snow is still falling. . . ."

"Howie!" said Mrs. Lindeman.

"Right," I said. "I'll stay awhile when my mom brings us back."

Nathan elbowed me when we got in the car. He offered me free advice because we're best friends.

"Well, actually, Howie, you should get two or three somebodies to help. You have fifteen customers, right?"

"Well, more like eleven now."

"Get help soon, Howie, before you're down to zero."

I was a little concerned about the contest rules.

"Why?" asked Nathan. "Paige and I worked together. I'm sure it's okay if you hire some employees."

"You and Paige are partners?" I asked.

"For the Stocking Stuffer Gift Coupons. Remember?" he said. "We're selling them tonight outside Santa's Workshop."

Nathan flipped through the book of coupons I *thought* had been Paige's idea. Nathan read my coupon that had a picture of a snowflake.

"'Leave no snowflake unshoveled,'" he read. "'Call A Boy for All Seasons.' You're offering three dollars off, Howie, on a customer's first snow removal job? Maybe," said Nathan, "make that four somebodies."

Howard J. Fingerhut's $ecret #5: Hire People You Know

Mrs. Muckley had been Mr. Muckley's very first employee at the Muckley Milkshakes on the Turnpike.

"My H. Marion hired people he knew," she told us.

I'm not married so I did the next best thing. I hired Brendan, Jed, Ned, and Tony Jr.

The five of us have been friends since nursery school *and* we play on the same soccer, basketball, and baseball teams. Well, four of us do. Brendan brings the balls and drinks.

"This way everybody wins," I told them after Santa's Workshop closed. We were sitting in the last booth at Muckley's off the Square along with Spenser, who had pulled up a chair. The peppermint sundaes were Mrs. Muckley's treat.

Brendan began swiping the cherries from each of our sundaes.

"What do you mean, 'everybody wins,' Howie?" Brendan asked. "You want us to shovel for you for $1.50 an hour!"

"Well, $1.50 is better than nothing," I said. I took back my cherry. "I hear Snacks-a-Go-Go went bye-bye last week."

"Yeah," yelled Spenser. "He ate up his profits!"

Brendan picked off the cherry I'd put back on my sundae. "I might get a loan from Elliott in January."

"How about making it seven dollars an hour?" Tony Jr. asked. He covered his sundae so Brendan couldn't reach it.

"Sorry, Tony," I said. "Amber told me you're losing money, too. No one's taking skateboarding lessons with snow on the ground."

"Well, how about six dollars?" Jed asked.

"People don't get cars washed in a snowstorm, Jed."

"Then maybe five dollars?"

"Or bikes washed either, Ned. I'll pay three bucks an hour," I said, "and you use your own shovels, but I'll throw in hot chocolate—"

"With marshmallows?" Brendan asked.

"Probably," I said.

Spenser swiped Brendan's cherry. "Heh, heh, heh. Not if you don't collect from *your* customers, Fingerhut. Remember that collection problem you won't hire me to fix?"

"My collection problem is almost gone, Spenser. It was very slight. And I don't remember asking you to sit at this table."

"Wait a minute. What does *slight* mean?" Brendan asked. "What if we shovel and you don't have money to pay us?"

"Trust me," I said. "I'm piling up the profits."

Spenser laughed his Spenser laugh. "Heh, heh, heh. Piling up the profits? Elliott told Amber you're digging yourself in deeper."

For one dollar, I hired Mike McQuire to take a Mike-Moments Instant Photo of me and my new employees shaking hands at the downtown Muckley's.

"This is definitely a Mike-Moment," Mike said. "At the count of three, everyone yell, '*Shovel!*'"

I'll tell my publisher to print the photo in this chapter, once I pay Mike and he gives me the photo. Just remember, Spenser *isn't* an employee.

Howard J. Fingerhut's $ecret #6: Spend Time with Your Employees

Mrs. Muckley told us she knows every Muckley employee personally.

"We're one big happy family," Mrs. Muckley said.

So on the day after the third snowstorm, which happened to be a Sunday, I invited Brendan, Jed, Ned, and Tony Jr. to bring their shovels to Grandma Millie's house.

"We'll shovel the Kupfermans together," I explained when we met out front at ten o'clock. "I'll show you how to shovel and give you some tips."

"We're talking about shoveling," Tony said. "I think we can handle it."

Jed and Ned stuffed a snowball down my ski jacket.

"This is serious, guys. I'm running a business."

"Lighten up," said Brendan. "And where's the hot chocolate?"

"You'll get your hot chocolate when we finish up on Maple."

Grandma Millie said we were better than a snowplow. I did the front and back walks. Brendan did the sidewalks. Jed, Ned, and Tony Jr. shoveled the driveways. We shoveled down to the cement. We left wide paths for walking. We piled the snow in very neat mounds.

We took two breaks. One was on Elm, when we finished the walk to Dr. Richards's dentist office. We built a snowman underneath his tooth sign. The other was on Oak, when we finished Reverend Wick's. Spenser came by and challenged us to a snowball fight.

All of my customers thanked me for prompt and friendly service.

Four of my customers paid me when we finished. It turns out most of my customers prefer end-of-the-month billing.

"Just send us the bill, Howie, and we'll pay by the third."

My walks-and-driveway combo rate was fifteen dollars. Minus three dollars with the first-time Winter Wonderland coupon.

"So where's *our* money?" Brendan asked. We were back at Grandma Millie's, drinking hot chocolate.

Tony put out his hand. "Remember?" he said. "Three bucks an hour!"

"It's two o'clock," said Jed.

"You owe us twelve bucks each," said Ned.

"I'm thinking of paying my employees by the month," I explained.

Brendan suggested I think again. Jed, Ned, and Tony Jr. stood up and made the same suggestion.

"On the other hand," I said, "I could pay you by the day. . . ."

I have now spent four snowstorms shoveling with my workers. I am confident they can handle any storm that comes their way.

Oh, and they can also handle subzero temperatures. I had Grandma Millie knit them orange mufflers for Christmas.

Hoe! Hoe! Hoe! from A Boy for All Seasons Lawn Care!

(Paige thought that up for my holiday greeting card.)

Chapter Five
January

If you're ever having problems running your business, January is a good month to wipe the slate clean.

Mrs. Muckley said so when she spoke to us last week.

So did my parents and my grandma Millie.

This January rule applies even to someone like me who has been New and Improved since last summer.

"There's always room for improvement, Howie," my mom said about three days after the Arctic Clipper shut down Mt. Olive.

"And maybe," my dad said, "you're not as new as you think."

Mrs. Muckley said, "Mistakes happen, Howie. Be honest with your customers. Be honest with your employees. Just put it in writing and be sure to keep a copy."

I'll tell my publisher to print my correspondence here. Notice the many ways you can communicate with your employees and customers.

Oh, and your friends and family and neighbors and City Hall.

In case you're wondering, you-know-who gave me the stationery. She picked my name for the Secret Santa.

To: BigBrendan@mt.olive4cornersrobedeaux.edu
SuperTonyJr@mt.olive4cornersrobedeaux.edu
Jed-o-TheGreat@mt.olive4cornersrobedeaux.edu
Ned-o-TheGreat@mt.olive4cornersrobedeaux.edu

From: Howie@mt.olive4cornersrobedeaux.edu

Date: January 7

SUBJECT: Your Arctic Clipper Shoveling

Can you believe that we had two snow days off from school?!

I'm glad I could count on you to shovel my customers' front and back paths and sidewalks while my dad and I cleaned my customers' driveways.

Weren't we lucky Mr. Busghetti lent my dad and me his snowblower?

Are you sure you counted up your hours right? Sixteen hours seems like a lot.

I'll see you at tomorrow's game. My shooting arm's in great shape thanks to all this shoveling.

Oh, and we won't be shoveling for Reverend Wick or Dr. Richards anymore.

—Howie

A BOY FOR ALL SEASONS LAWN CARE SERVICE
Howard J. Fingerhut, President
2408 Maple
Mt. Olive, MO 63303

January 8

Dr. Richards
2106 Elm
Mt. Olive, MO 63303

Dear Dr. Richards:

I'm sorry about your tooth sign.

I know all of my workers. I spend a lot of time with them. They never put grape jelly inside any of their snowballs. Whoever told you they did was probably the person who threw the snowballs. Does the person who told you this live behind you on Oak?

You owe me $15.00 for the Arctic Clipper job *plus* $90.00 for my December shoveling *plus* $10.00 for your November raking. Remember how you told me the check was in the mail?

Spring isn't that far away. Maybe you'll rehire A Boy for All Seasons for your spring cleanup.

Sincerely,

Howard J. Fingerhut
President
A Boy for All Seasons Lawn Care Service

A BOY FOR ALL SEASONS LAWN CARE SERVICE
Howard J. Fingerhut, President
2408 Maple
Mt. Olive, MO 63303

January 8

Reverend and Mrs. Wick
2206 Elm
Mt. Olive, MO 63303

Dear Reverend and Mrs. Wick:

I'm sorry about your tulip bulbs. I know you special-ordered them from Holland. I'm sure they would have looked nice along your walk.

Due to the eight-foot-high drifts of snow, some of my workers had a hard time finding the *exact* front paths to shovel. Don't most people plant gardens in the back?

When you get your new tulip bulbs, think about rehiring A Boy for All Seasons. We'll probably have a spring cleanup/planting special.

You owe me $15.00 for the Arctic Clipper shoveling job plus $10.00 for your fall raking.

Sincerely,

Howard J. Fingerhut
President
A Boy for All Seasons Lawn Care Service

From the desk of Howard J. Fingerhut

January 8

To whom it may concern:

(1) You don't need to give me any of the plant mulch you're making from people's dead Christmas trees and wreaths. I'll buy some on sale at Alexander Hardware in March.

(2) Never come near me with mistletoe again!

(3) I'm using the stationery.

To: BigBrendan@mt.olive4cornersrobedeaux.edu
SuperTonyJr@mt.olive4cornersrobedeaux.edu
Jed-o-TheGreat@mt.olive4cornersrobedeaux.edu
Ned-o-TheGreat@mt.olive4cornersrobedeaux.edu

From: Howie@mt.olive4cornersrobedeaux.edu

Date: January 15

SUBJECT: Where were you guys?

You were supposed to meet me at Mrs. Kupferman's after school today to shovel the latest snow.

Where were you guys?

I shoveled the walks of as many customers as I could (3). My dad and I cleaned 3 driveways after dinner.

I have at least 2 customers who still need shoveling.

Meet me tomorrow on the playground at 8.
—Howie

A BOY FOR ALL SEASONS LAWN CARE SERVICE
Howard J. Fingerhut, President
2408 Maple
Mt. Olive, MO 63303

January 16

Mr. Mitch Montgomery
2356 Thornwood
Mt. Olive, MO 63303

Dear Mr. Montgomery:

I'm sorry about your car.

My dad and I did not know you parked your Bug on the other side of Mrs. Kupferman's bushes. When we came to clean *your* driveway, we thought the big mound of snow was maybe an igloo. A lot of people are building igloos this winter.

My mom can pick you up if you need a ride to Saturday's game. We know what happened won't affect your calls. Ha! Ha!

Maybe you can bring the $30.00 you owe me?

Sincerely,

Howard J. Fingerhut
President
A Boy for All Seasons Lawn Care Service

A BOY FOR ALL SEASONS LAWN CARE SERVICE
Howard J. Fingerhut, President
2408 Maple
Mt. Olive, MO 63303

January 18

Mr. Frank Busghetti
2121 Oak
Mt. Olive, MO 63303

Dear Mr. Busghetti:

I'm sorry about your snowblower.

My dad and I took it to Alexander Hardware today to see if it can be fixed.

Mr. Alexander checked and the warranty hasn't expired yet.

It's only three months old so the problem can't be that big.

Sincerely,

Howard J. Fingerhut
President
A Boy for All Seasons Lawn Care Service

P.S. Thanks for lending us the snowblower.

January 20

Dear Paige,

    I like your spring ad for A Boy for All Seasons—
"Leave no blade uncut!"

    I think it's very catchy.

    I see that you raised your rates. Maybe we can
meet at the mall next Sunday and talk about my
spring advertising campaign?

    Amber told me you're tied with Nathan in The
Contest.

    Congratulations!

Howie

$ $ $ $ $ $ $ $ $ $ $ $ $ $ $ $ $ $ $
MONEY PROBLEMS?
NEED MONEY FAST?
START OFF THE YEAR WITH
MONEY TO SPARE
Phone Mi$terBuck$ today.
Your cash will be flowing.
888-555-4567
or
Drop this card in your nearest mailbox.
(   )   Yes, I'd like to borrow money at a low,
friendly rate.

Name   Howard J. Fingerhut
Address   2408 Maple, Mt. Olive, MO 63303
Business   A Boy for All Seasons
Phone   555-4494
e-mail   Howie@mt.olive4cornersrobedeaux.edu

I'm interested in never, ever doing business with you!
No matter what Amber says. I do not have a cash-
flow problem!
Howard J. Fingerhut

To: BigBrendan@mt.olive4cornersrobedeaux.edu
SuperTonyJr@mt.olive4cornersrobedeaux.edu
Jed-o-TheGreat@mt.olive4cornersrobedeaux.edu
Ned-o-TheGreat@mt.olive4cornersrobedeaux.edu

From: Howie@mt.olive4cornersrobedeaux.edu

Date: January 22

SUBJECT: How dumb do you think I am?

Sure you had strep throat last week!

Today's *Mt. Olive Gazette* has a front-page picture of 4 boys sledding down Centennial Hill on the afternoon of January 15.

All of them are wearing the exact same muffler!

Don't show up when it snows again. I'm planning to hire Luis and his brother.

Sincerely,

Howard J. Fingerhut
President
A Boy for All Seasons Lawn Care Service

A BOY FOR ALL SEASONS LAWN CARE SERVICE
Howard J. Fingerhut, President
2408 Maple
Mt. Olive, MO 63303

January 23

The Department of Streets
The Village of Mt. Olive
525 Central
Mt. Olive, MO 63303

Dear Madam or Sir:

I am the president of A Boy for All Seasons Lawn Care Service.

I shovel snow for people on Thornwood, Oak, Elm, and Maple.

Could you please ask your snowplow drivers to *not dump the snow* so it blocks my customer's driveways? Three of my customers think I didn't do my job.

Also, your drivers sometimes dump the snow in high piles on the *sides* of the driveways. This makes backing out of the drive-ways very dangerous. Isn't this against the law?

Thank you.

Howard J. Fingerhut
President
A Boy for All Seasons Lawn Care Service

A BOY FOR ALL SEASONS LAWN CARE SERVICE

To: Spenser Baggey
From: Howard J. Fingerhut
Date: January 24

I told you this yesterday, but I'm putting it in writing:

(1) Guardian Angels, Inc., is NOT the answer to my prayers.

(2) DON'T GO ANYWHERE NEAR MY LAWN CARE CUSTOMERS!

(3) Amber and Elliott don't know what they're talking about.

(4) I know it was you who decked Dr. Richards's tooth sign.

(5) I can't come to your sleepover. I'm going to Iowa with my mom to do research for her pig jokes.

Howard J. Fingerhut

Chapter Six
February

February is short and so is this chapter.

I'll tell my publisher to print my President's Day interview with Mrs. Muckley. (I used my new CD player/tape recorder, and Grandma Millie typed it up.) The interview was part of my "On the Job with a Mt. Olive Senior Businessperson" report I handed in yesterday. Don't expect any Mike-Moments Instant Photos. I still owe him for my November and December photos plus he raised his prices just before Valentine's Day.

At the end of the chapter I'll include a confe$$ion.

Oh, and maybe my horoscope and Vince's spring weather forecast and February's Mt. Olive Park District basketball scores if they're in the sports section of today's *Mt. Olive Gazette.*

On the Job with Mrs. H. Marion Muckley

HJF: I liked following you around today at Muckley's off the Square. I learned a lot about how to run a business. Even if customers weren't lining up, I thought your George Washington Cherry Ice-Cream Soda Special was a good idea.

MM: Thank you, Howie. It was a pleasure showing you the ropes.

HJF: Oh, and thanks for the five extra *MOOLA-MOOLA* Sweepstakes cards *and* the free caramel sundae.

MM: Caramel was Mr. Muckley's favorite topping.

HJF: Speaking of Mr. Muckley, I'm curious about his grass-cutting business and his early years as a junior businessperson.

MM: My H. Marion was a businessperson from the day he was born! He'd think up one clever business idea after another, and he was always so eager.

HJF: I'm like that, too, Mrs. Muckley! I wrote a name poem and my *E* was for *enthusiastic*. Did his parents encourage him?

MM: They couldn't do enough to help their son grow his ideas. He was an only child, you know.

HJF: Really?

MM: Really. Can I get you another sundae?

HJF: Thank you. Maybe later. Is there anything you can tell me about Mr. Muckley's school days?

MM: Between you and me, Howie, my grand-daughter's just like him. Quiet but deter-mined. And very smart.

HJF: I can't believe this. My *I* is for *intelligent*!

MM: Of course, sometimes he was too smart for his own good. At least that's what the other boys and girls said. They didn't take him seriously.

HJF: You might find this hard to believe, but some people don't take me seriously either. In fact, someone changed my name poem *O* to *out of his mind*. What did Mr. Muckley do?

MM: He ignored them and kept working.

HJF: Did Mr. Muckley have any businessperson success secrets? I'm writing a book that has many of *my* businessperson $ecret$, but I could add a chapter just for Mr. Muckley's.

MM: I know about your book, Howie. My grand-
daughter told me. And my H. Marion had
three success secrets. His first success secret
was he worked very hard.

HJF: He didn't play sports or go on trips with his
parents or go to summer sports camp or
hang out with his grandma?

MM: He worked all day, every day, all year long. If
he'd written a name poem, his *H* would have
been *hardworking.*

HJF: Mine's for *hopeful,* and I'll take that other
sundae.

MM: Caramel, again?

HJF: I think I'll try the cherry special. What was
Mr. Muckley's second success secret?

MM: My H. Marion never gave up.

HJF: What if he had a *slight* collection problem
that sort of snowballed?

MM: My H. Marion would hire a bill collector.

HJF: What if he couldn't serve all of his customers
because of a weather disaster beyond his
control like, oh, let's say, an Arctic Clipper?

MM: He'd hire extra help and they'd all work
overtime.

HJF: What if his expenses were almost as high as
his income?

MM: He'd borrow money from the Throop Bank of Missouri.

HJF: And if four of his employees started their own drive-up ice-cream business and stole his customers?

MM: He'd think up new and better desserts.

HJF: Just like me! My *O* is for *original*! Now I clean windshields and salt driveways and sidewalks and brush snow off cars at the Mt. Olive mall! What was Mr. Muckley's third success secret?

MM: My H. Marion was willing to take risks. For instance, he opened this Muckley Milkshakes off the Square and it *isn't* a drive up.

HJF: The *W* in my Howie poem stands for *willing*! In fact, guess who used his last ten dollars to play your Muckley Milkshakes *MOOLA-MOOLA* Sweepstakes?

MM: For goodness' shakes! Isn't that a little *too* risky?

HJF: I don't think so. Thanks to Grandma Millie and a certain person I'm not mentioning, I have every single game piece to spell "*MOOLA-MOOLA!*"

MM: Including the exclamation point?

HJF: Including the exclamation point. Once I get the hyphen, I'll win twenty-five hundred dollars!

MM: My, my! Shakes alive!

HJF: Would you be interested in writing an endorsement for my book, once I win The Contest, of course, and sell the book to my publisher?

MM: It would be my pleasure. You know, my granddaughter's growing flowers from those seeds of hers. You could plant them for your customers in the spring and she said she wouldn't charge you.

HJF: Maybe some of my mom's cow jokes might beef up your sales. Ha! Ha! See you later, Mrs. Muckley.

Howard J. Fingerhut's Confe$$ion #2

In case you forgot the formula, here it is again.

$75.00 (A Boy for All Season's winter income)
− $69.57 (A Boy for All Season's winter expenses)
───
$5.43 (A Boy for All Season's winter profit)

Thanks to my "on the job" visit with Mrs. Muckley, I am not concerned that A Boy for All Seasons made only a small profit this winter.

Spring is just around the corner. Rain makes grass grow. And twenty-five hundred dollars is a whole lot of green!

I have one season left to win The Contest, no matter what Amber says her crystal ball predicts.

Forecast for March

Sagittarius (Nov. 21 to Dec. 20)
All signs point to financial success. Cycle high. The ball's in your court. Check for water problems.

Spring Weather Forecast

Meteorologist Vince Jerome, from WMTO, predicts an unusually rainy spring with record-breaking rain-falls for most of Missouri.

Oh, and just in case you're interested:

MT. OLIVE PARK
DISTRICT BASKETBALL FINALS
Pony League
Buccaneers 45, Cavaliers 40
(high scores: Buccaneers—
Fingerhut 12, McQuire 10)

Chapter Seven
March

I'm off to Lake of the Ozarks tomorrow for my dad's Missouri History Teachers Convention.

I've decided to pack my new pitcher's glove. I'll be playing baseball again—when the rain stops—on Paige's father's team, Alexander Hardware. I'm thinking of pitching instead of playing shortstop this season.

Here are three more important business $ecret$.

Oh, and the front page from last week's *Mt. Olive Gazette.*

I've phoned Mrs. Muckley five times. Each time her secretary says, "She's not available for comment."

CUSTOMERS ALL SHOOK UP
OVER MUCKLEY MILKSHAKES
SWEEPSTAKES SCANDAL

*Company Admits Failure to Print
Winning Hyphen Game Piece*

RAIN, RAIN, GO AWAY!

Mt. Olive's March rains should break the record

Howard J. Fingerhut's $ecret #7: Learn to Accept Criticism

I stopped by Nathan's the day I learned about the *MOOLA-MOOLA* Sweepstakes scandal.

Mrs. Lindeman opened the door. "How come you're here, Howie? It's raining cats and dogs."

I unbuckled my slicker and took out an appointment card. "I have a 2 P.M. appointment with Dr. Homework."

"Paige and Nathan are in the family room."

"Paige *and* Nathan?" I asked.

Paige *and* Nathan were very busy counting the money they'd made from their St. Patrick's Day Little Green Book o' Coupons special.

When Paige saw me, she flipped back her hair and pushed it behind her ears.

"You know, that was a shame, Howie, about the Muckley Milkshakes hyphen scandal. Amber told me you lost your last ten dollars."

"I'm a lucky Sagittarian, no matter *what* Amber says. And I need to speak to Nathan. In private," I added.

"Well, actually," Nathan said, "now that Mrs. Muckley and Ms. Robedeaux said we could merge our contest businesses, Paige and I are business partners."

Paige flipped back her hair.

"That way, Howie, Dr. Homework and I are pretty hard to beat. I'm working on our business name. We want something catchy."

I got to the point.

"I want my money back, Nathan, for last October's Junior Businessperson IQ Test!" I showed him my test paper. "According to your evaluation, I should be winning The Contest."

I showed him my Personal Interests answer. "Anything that has to do with sports."

I showed him my Skills answer. "Anything that has to do with sports."

I showed him my Talents answer. "Anything that has to do with sports."

I showed him my Job Experience answer. "Raking and snow shoveling."

"You said lawn care, Nathan, was the perfect fit!"

Nathan and Paige studied the next few pages.

Paige whispered in Nathan's ear. He whispered back.

"Well, actually," Nathan said to me, "it *was* the perfect fit. I think there's a problem with your *other* answers. You checked 'yes' when you should have checked 'no.'"

I looked at the first question. "I'm healthy," I said. "I certainly don't have the chicken pox like Mike and Luis."

"Well, actually," said Nathan, "it's questions five through eight."

Paige read question number five out loud. "'Before beginning a project, you stop, think, and *then* you act.'"

Nathan said, "Remember your pet-sitting service, Howie, and the Kupfermans' Chihuahuas?"

"I'm New and Improved now, Nathan. That was second grade."

Paige read number six. "'You finish what you start.'"

Nathan said, "Remember the popcorn balls, Howie, you were supposed to sell at the Park District games?"

"That was third grade, Nathan, and I'd never cooked before."

Paige read number seven. "'You take criticism well.'"

"I do," I said.

"Not!" said Nathan. "You always have an excuse, Howie, why something went wrong, and it's never your fault, in case you hadn't noticed."

"What does number eight say?" I asked.

"'You're open to other people's ideas,'" Paige read. "You know, this might be a 'yes' answer, Nathan. Howie always listens very carefully whenever I talk to him about his advertising plan."

"Which reminds me," I said, "you gave 'Leave no blade uncut' to Jed and Ned! And you gave them my business name. They're 'Two Boys for Two Seasons.'"

"Truth in advertising is very important, Howie. And the truth is, you're not a boy for all seasons anymore. Besides, you know, I'm running a business."

"Well, I am, too!" I said. "Yesterday I signed up my first commercial grass-cutting account—Mrs. Kettlestring's Ye Olde Candy Shoppe. Tomorrow I'm bidding on the Lovejoy Bed and Breakfast. I've been pricing power mowers at your father's March Madness Sale. Oh, and I'm scheduling a demonstration of my clipping and edging services at my grandma Millie's after spring vacation."

Paige whispered in Nathan's ear. Nathan whispered back.

"If you're willing to listen," Nathan said to me, "we have an idea: you should merge with Muckley Greens and Seeds."

"You could call yourselves A Boy and a Girl for at Least Two Seasons," Paige said. "Catchy, don't you think?"

"No," I said. "Any more ideas since that one's never happening?"

They looked at each other.

"Well, actually," said Nathan, "Mi$terBuck$ would lend you money."

"And hiring Spenser," Paige said, "is a good idea, too. Everybody's using him. Even us."

She smiled at Nathan. Nathan blushed.

Nathan returned the $2.50 I paid him for my Junior Businessperson IQ Test.

"But you still owe me five dollars for today's visit," he said.

Paige shook out her hair, then pushed it back behind her ears. "You know, we're running a business, Howie."

"Bill me," I said.

Howard J. Fingerhut's $ecret #8: Be Open to Other People's Ideas

Nathan and Paige were wrong about question number eight. I am *very* open to new ideas.

In fact, last Tuesday, during indoor recess, I met Elliott in the reading corner to arrange for a loan from Mi$terBuck$. Just like Mr. Muckley, I like personal contact.

It turns out, I had to wait in line. Tony Jr. was ahead of me and Mike was ahead of him.

All three of us got the same deal:

(1) instant on-the-spot cash (in my case, $50.00);

(2) low, easy monthly payments;

(3) no payment due for two months!

Oh, and

(4) only 25 percent interest, payable each month.

I read the small print on Elliott's loan agreement and signed my name in cursive on the dotted line.

"What happens if, let's say, oh, I don't know, I'm busy and I can't stop cutting grass to come by to pay you the first $12.50 payment on May 21."

"No problem," Elliott said. "I hired Guardian Angel, Inc. Spenser will find you wherever you are."

"To collect my monthly payment?"

"Plus the $12.50 interest," Elliott said. "You're my fourth new customer today, Howie, and it's not even lunchtime." He punched in numbers on his tiny calculator. "Business is picking up. I could win this contest."

I waved my ten Abe Lincolns in front of Elliott's glasses.

"Don't call me 'Howie' and don't be so sure."

Howard J. Fingerhut's $ecret #9: Stop, Think, and *Then* Act

This afternoon before science, Spenser put out his foot and stopped me in the hall.

He said, "Amber told me you're looking for a bill collector. She said you lost your last ten bucks in the *MOOLA-MOOLA* Sweepstakes."

He pointed to his name poem, which happened to be above us. Ms. Robedeaux insisted that the poems stay up all year.

"I'm *strong,* Fingerhut, like the first *S* says. And check out the *R.* *R* stands for *reliable,*" he said. "Guardian Angel, Inc., is the answer to your prayers."

I thought a minute. Nine customers still owed me $296.15. I needed that money to win The Contest.

On the other hand, *really tough* was a good *R* choice for Spenser.

I looked at Spenser's poem. The second *S* said *speedy.*

Finally I acted. I gave him the names and addresses of three of my delinquent customers on Elm—the Moxleys, the Duckworths, and Dr. Richards.

"This is only a trial run," I said, "for only these three customers. Don't even *think* of ringing the Busghettis' front doorbell."

"Why not come with me, Fingerhut, and

watch me close-up? You could learn a few things, like how to be tough."

"My customers," I said, "are used to service with a smile."

"That's your problem, Fingerhut. My customers aren't."

I reminded Spenser to give receipts to my customers.

Spenser reminded *me* I owed him fifteen dollars. "Five bucks per house," he said. "Cash up front only."

"Maybe you could bill me?"

"Heh, heh, heh."

I stopped. I thought. I handed him three fives.

Chapter Eight
April

Vince was right. This morning he reported on his Live-at-Five Farmers Report that the rain would break as early as lunchtime. It's almost noon and I don't feel a drop! I'm off with my mower to Ye Olde Candy Shoppe.

I hope Mrs. Muckley was right, too. At the spring open house last week, she announced the new Muckley Milkshakes *MOOLA-MOOLA* game piece policy: one free milkshake for each *MOOLA-MOOLA* game piece left over from the February sweepstakes. She said, "My H. Marion believed mistakes are good. No one ever succeeds without making a few mistakes."

Amber said she heard a lot of parents complaining that Mrs. Muckley's contest was the biggest mistake of the school year. She said Crissy Mull's mom said Ms. Robedeaux was too young to teach. She said Julianna Schlossberg's dad said Ms. Robedeaux should be fired. She said Monica's stepmother said, "Running a business is not one of the three R's."

I think Ms. Robedeaux has some good ideas. This month she let *us* write the word problems for our Word Problem Workout. We used real and personal facts from our contest businesses.

Businesspeople solve word problems all the time. I'll tell my publisher to print my Word Problem Workout right here so you can practice for when *you're* a businessperson. I'll leave plenty of work space and ask my publisher to print the correct answers upside down at the end of each chapter. Make sure you double-check your work and label your answers. (Ha! Ha!)

Howard J. Fingerhut's Junior Businessperson Word Problem Workout

1. I now charge $15.00 to mow a regular-size lawn, back and front. If it stops raining tonight, April 30, and it doesn't rain again until The Contest ends on June 14, how much money will I earn mowing two lawns each day, every day, between now and June 14—assuming my new customers on Pine and Walnut pay me and they have their own Mt. Olive Village bags for grass clippings?

answer: $1350.00

2. Last night Grandma Millie measured 1 foot of rainwater in her basement. If two of her neighbors measured 8 inches of rainwater, one of her neighbors measured 11 inches of rainwater, and three of her neighbors measured 15 inches of rainwater, what was the average amount of rainwater in the basements of Grandma Millie's neighbors on Thornwood?

answer: 12 inches

3. Spenser collected $15.00 from Mrs. Moxley, $12.00 from Mr. Duckworth, and a check for $97.00 from Dr. Richards. The Throop Bank of Missouri wouldn't honor the check, and Spenser broke the Busghettis' front doorbell, which cost me $35.00 to fix. How much money am I out since Spenser began collecting for me?

answer: $8.00

4. In September, Mrs. Muckley gave each of Ms. Robedeaux's 20 students $50.00 to start a contest business. If 8 other businesses besides mine are down to zero, how much money has Mrs. Muckley lost so far?

answer: $450.00

5. When a person has the chicken pox, he's supposed to take 1 teaspoon of anti-itch medicine for each 25 pounds he weighs. Brendan weighs 100 pounds. How many teaspoons of anti-itch medicine should Brendan take tonight?

answer: 4 teaspoons

6. It takes 11 to 21 days for a person to break out with the chicken pox after he's been exposed. If it's true what my dad says—that kids are the most contagious the day before they break out with a rash—and I rode with Brendan to Jed and Ned's pizza party yesterday, April 29, what is the earliest day next month I could break out with the chicken pox? What is the latest day I could break out with the chicken pox?

Answers: May 9 and May 19

7. If it's April 30 and I used up my $50.00 loan paying Spenser and Alexander Hardware, how many days left do I have to earn the $25.00 I'm supposed to pay Elliott on May 21?

Answer: 21 days

98

Chapter Nine
May

Here is my third confe$$ion.

It might be my last. A Boy for All Seasons earned minus $40.00 this spring.

Howard J. Fingerhut's Confe$$ion #3

Today is May 19 and I am writing this chapter in the best hiding place a boy could find—the second-floor girls' room of the Four Corners School. I'm in the second stall from the window.

When I first came in, after the three o'clock bell rang, I was in the third stall. But I forgot to raise my feet when I heard Spenser run in.

He recognized my rain boots and opened the door.

"I do not have Mi$terBuck$'s twenty-five dollars!" I said. I reached into my backpack and pulled out a Muckley Milkshakes paper bag. "Here," I said. "How about thirty-three free milkshakes?"

Spenser wasn't interested in my bag of MOOLA-MOOLA game pieces. Instead he backed off and asked, "What's wrong with your face?"

I ran to the mirror on the wall above the sinks.

There were three red blotches, with little raised dots, on my right cheek. Two red blotches were on my left. I lifted up my Redbird Sports Camp T-shirt and checked my stomach. Little red blotches were starting to appear.

"Just what I needed!" I said. "Brendan's chicken pox!"

Spenser stepped back the whole length of the bathroom.

"According to my dad, Spenser, I was the most contagious yesterday."

"When we bowled on the same team at Nathan's birthday party?"

I remembered my word problems. "You've got eleven to twenty-one days."

I looked again at my face in the mirror.

"Perfect!" I said. "Each one's like a zero, which is just what I am. I'm A Boy for No Seasons! New and Improved? Ha! I'm my mom's biggest joke!"

I dragged out my backpack, reached for my how-to book, and then tossed it in the trash can. It was a perfect three-pointer.

"Hey!" said Spenser. "You threw away your book!"

"What book, Spenser?"

"That book, Fingerhut!"

"In order to have a book, Spenser, I have to have a publisher," I said. "But in order to have a publisher, I have to win The Contest. Of course, in order to win The Contest, I have to have a profit—the biggest profit. Guess what, Spenser?"

"You're a lucky Sagittarian?" Spenser asked.

"Between the rain and my loan payment and a certain bill collector, my profit for spring is *minus* forty bucks."

A clap of thunder shook the skylight above us.

"Just what we need," I said. "Another May rainstorm."

For somebody who was supposed to be a bully, Spenser surprised me. He dug down into the trash bin and removed my book. Then he paged through the chapters, looking for his name. Every time he found it, he said, "Yeah! That's me!"

Spenser especially liked my $ecret$ and confe$$ion$.

"This place is empty, right? It's just you and me?" He looked all around, even under the fourth stall that had been locked when I came in. "I know a secret nobody knows."

"Even Amber?" I asked. I was checking for chicken pox under my arms.

"Even Little Miss Big Mouth. Heh, heh, heh. Nathan and Paige and Elliott are broke."

I instantly stopped scratching. "You're kidding," I said.

"Un-ah," Spenser answered. "Everybody owes everybody, but nobody's paying. Everyone's broke. Oh, except for your girlfriend who kissed you last field day."

I ignored his remark. "You're broke, too?"

"Yeah. I'm broke, too. You were the only one who paid me last month."

A bolt of lightning flashed across the skylight. I waited for the thunderclap and scratched my stomach.

My mind began writing a very interesting word problem. *If Howie's last chicken pox scabs on May 27, which means he'd have 17 days left to mow and mulch, and if it doesn't rain and he can dig up some new customers, how much money can Howie earn to win The Contest and sell his book?*

Meanwhile, water hit my head. Rain was coming through the skylight.

"Ms. Robedeaux picked the wrong theme," said Spenser. He was getting wet, too. "She should have picked rain. . . ."

I remembered my February horoscope. "Or maybe drowning," I said.

"Yeah. We're all going under. Heh, heh, heh."

"Ms. Robedeaux, too," I said. "And maybe Mrs. Muckley."

Right then my mind rewrote my Mrs. Muckley word problem.

In September, Mrs. Muckley gave each of Ms. Robedeaux's 20 students $50.00 to start a contest business. If 18 other businesses besides mine are down to zero, how much money has Mrs. Muckley lost so far?

I did the math. $950.00.

By this time, Spenser was busy studying the page with my name poem. I looked all around. It still was just the two of us.

"I have another confe$$ion," I said.

"Yeah?" asked Spenser.

"Yeah," I said. "I planned to change my *I* word when my book was published."

"To what?" Spenser asked.

"To *important*," I answered. "But now Amber's right. I'm an idiot, Spenser."

"What does she know? She reads tea leaves and palms. You wrote this book, didn't you?"

"Just chapters one through eight."

Spenser finished reading my Personal Message.

"Maybe," he said, "while you're home itching, *you* should read your book. Heh, heh, heh. It says right here you'll learn how to run a business."

"Wait a minute, Spenser. That's not a dumb idea. . . ."

"Yeah?" asked Spenser.

"Yeah," I said. "Maybe one of your *S*'s, Spenser, could stand for *smart*."

"So you still could win The Contest and still could sell your book?"

My *H* was for *hopeful*.

"Sure," I said. "Well, maybe," I added. I scratched the pox on my right and left ears.

"Then do me a favor." He showed me my Note to the Reader. "Don't change my name. I've never been in a book."

Once Spenser left, I made myself comfortable. I took out my book and wrote, "Chapter Nine . . ."

Chapter Ten
June

Today is June 15 and this is the very last chapter of my how-to book.

A lot has happened since I wrote Chapter Nine.

First, fourteen other people caught Brendan's chicken pox—including Nathan, Paige, Spenser, and Elliott.

Oh, and Mr. Busghetti. He was bowling one lane over at Nathan's birthday party.

Second, I took Spenser's advice. While my chicken pox scabbed, I read my how-to book twice.

That is why today I won the H. Marion Muckley Junior Businessperson of the Year

Contest! (Of course, so did nineteen other students in Ms. Robedeaux's class.) I also accepted the Junior Businessperson of the Year trophy! (Of course, I accepted it on *behalf* of those nineteen other students.) At this afternoon's Mt. Olive Chamber of Commerce Ceremony, Mrs. Muckley said, "You're a winner, Howie!"

Forget what Amber says. I'm my first satisfied customer.

Why Howard J. Fingerhut Recommends His Own Book

My how-to book taught me everything I needed to know to start and run the Fir$t Annual Mt. Olive/Four Corner$ $chool Garage $ale–Field Day–Lawn Event. My class held it five days ago at the Four Corners School. The profit was so big, we were even on TV. I'll tell my publisher to print the newspaper headline here.

Lawn Event Draws Record-breaking Crowds
Organizers Donate $5,778.00 to Help Sick Children

When I dreamed up this event, my life was like a nightmare.

My mom kept telling chicken jokes and doing the Chicken Dance.

She said, "A good laugh cures anything, Howie, even the chicken pox."

My dad kept insisting, "History can teach us."

Grandma Millie kept reading me my late spring horoscope: "Dark clouds hover but you'll find the silver lining."

I personally thought the Star Lady needed glasses. The only thing I found were flowers on my doorstep. The card read, *"Grown with love—from Muckley Greens and Seeds."*

I was reading my book a second time when my mom clucked by wearing her old shiny high school prom jacket. She'd found it in a trunk she'd brought up from the basement. Like everybody else's, our basement had flooded.

"Maybe the Senior Citizens Club will have another garage sale, Howie."

She flapped her elbows and pretended to fly. The inside of her jacket shimmered and glittered.

"The Star Lady was right!" I screamed. "I found my silver lining!"

In two seconds flat, I was dialing Nathan.

"Garage sale, Nathan!" I shouted into the telephone. "Ms. Robedeaux's class can sponsor a garage sale! We'll sell our contest products and services, too, plus rent out tables for folks to sell *their* stuff!"

"Well, actually," Nathan said, "that's an excellent idea."

Nathan was a little concerned, though, about the garage space.

"We'll just *call* it a garage sale," I explained. "We'll use the Four Corners School field and hold it on Field Day! Vince said a dry spell is due the first of June."

Nathan had one more concern.

"Well, actually," Nathan said, "maybe *I* should be in charge. Remember your score on the Junior Businessperson IQ Test?"

"You said lawn care, Nathan, fits my skills and talents. I'm calling this a Lawn Event. I'll call you tomorrow."

One minute later, my telephone rang.

"You know, Howie," the voice said, "Nathan just told me about your idea."

I wet down my hair part and scratched my right ear.

"Advertising, Howie, can make or break a garage sale. So I just wrote this slogan: 'Leave no item unsold.'"

"I was looking for something just a little bit catchier, Paige."

"With dollar signs, maybe?"

"Probably," I said.

"Okay, Howie. I'll get back to you tomorrow."

By the time Paige got back to me, I'd formed a VIP committee (that stands for Very Important People). My committee included Nathan (booth and table assignments), Spenser (security), Elliott (money boxes), and Paige (advertising). I'd also worked out the Lawn Event details with Mrs. Theodore, Ms. Robedeaux, Mrs. Muckley, and the Village.

Oh, and with the president of Muckley Greens and Seeds. She was waiting with flowers when I answered the door.

"Amber said that Monica said that Paige said that Nathan said that *you* thought up a plan to save my grandmother's contest! Oh, I knew you would, Howie! Your *H* should be for *Hero*!"

She offered me the flowers, but I moved two steps back.

"I'm probably still contagious. . . ."

"I had the chicken pox last summer, Howie."

Before I knew it, she'd moved three steps forward. My nose was in her daisies. Her foot was in my door.

She smiled at me, the same way she smiled at me at field day last year.

"You're such a good Idea Person, Howie! But you know what?" she asked. "I have hundreds of marigolds because of the rain. You could offer them for free to the first one hundred Lawn Event customers."

I tried to close the door. "Well, maybe," I said.

She smiled some more.

"And everybody knows you're the Lawn Care King, Howie! But you know what?" she asked. "My greens and seed business made my green thumb greener. I could mow your customers' lawns while you're away at sports camp."

My hand stayed on the doorknob. "Well, maybe," I said.

She smiled so wide I could see her back molars.

"And everybody but Amber says your book's a sure best-seller, Howie! But you know what?" she asked. "My grandmother and I are going to the restaurant convention in New York next week. A lot of publishers have offices there. I could drop off copies to help you find your publisher."

I opened the door. "How long can you stay?" I asked.

For the next half hour the two of us conducted business. I ordered one Muckley Greens and Seeds extra-large Thank-You Bouquet for Spenser. We reviewed my VIP committee and replaced Paige with a flower person. I copied my customer list, which didn't take long.

Oh, and both of us read through my how-to book.

At the end of Chapter Nine, the President of Muckley Greens and Seeds tapped me on the shoulder.

"That's Allyson," she said, "with two *l*s and a *y*."

"'Allyson,'" I said. "Two *l*s and a *y*."

Why Most of Howard J. Fingerhut's Classmates Recommend His Book

Eighteen of my classmates wanted to thank me for my great idea to organize the Fir$t Annual Mt. Olive/Four Corner$ $chool Garage $ale–Field Day–Lawn Event.

I remembered Mrs. Muckley's advice to put everything in writing.

"Maybe they could write a few words about my how-to book?" I suggested.

"Oh, Howie!" Allyson said. "You're such a good Idea Person!"

I had an even better idea while Allyson collected testimonials for my how-to book. Why not have my publisher print Mike's Mike-Moments Instant Photos of the Fir$t Annual Mt. Olive/Four Corner$ $chool Garage $ale–Field Day–Lawn Event right here in this chapter? That way my readers could actually *see* what happened when I used my own how-to book.

Most publishers print endorsements on the back cover anyway.

The VIP committee hired Mike to be the Official Photographer. I know that once I have a publisher, and once Mike and I agree to a reduced bill for my November and December photos, I'll be able to pay him the outrageous amount of money he's demanding if I want to include the following pictures.

Here are Reverend and Mrs. Wick beating out Nathan's mom for the free marigolds.

This is Mr. and Mrs. Busghetti arguing about the price of the snowblower they're selling.

This is Dr. Richards and the
tooth sign he's selling.

This is Coach Montgomery buying
my grandpa's car cover from
my grandma Millie.

This is Jed and Ned washing the
Kupfermans' two Chihuahuas.

Oh, and here's Amber reading Spenser's
palm for free! (She said his head line
shows he's smarter than people think.)

Speaking of Spenser,
here's a picture of Spenser
holding back the crowds
while Elliott makes change
for a twenty-dollar bill.

And here's a picture of Mrs. Theodore
holding back Spenser,
who's holding back the crowds
while Elliott makes change.

117

Guess who won the
Fourth-grade Fifty-yard Dash?
(Hint: his initials are HJF.)

And guess whose class won
the Fourth-grade Tug of War
when Spenser fell down and
Allyson took over? (Hint: the teacher's
name starts with an R and almost rhymes
with "Tokyo.")

It's hard to tell, but this is Brendan
and Tony Jr. hosing each other down
at Vince Jerome's
"Make Your Own Weather" booth.

And this is my mom and dad
inside the Muckley Moo cow suit,
selling Nathan and Paige an
"udderly funny joke" for $1.

Here's my class presenting a
Muckley Greens and Seeds
Thank-You Bouquet to Ms. Robedeaux.
The Mt. Olive School District
rehired her for next year.

Here's my class presenting a check
for $5,778.00 to Mrs. Muckley
for the boys and girls
at the Shriners Hospital.

Finally, this is me accepting
the H. Marion Muckley
Junior Businessperson of the Year trophy
from Mrs. Muckley at today's ceremony.
That's Allyson and my grandma Millie
leading the crowd in a wave.

Oh, and just in case you're interested.

MT. OLIVE PARK
DISTRICT BASEBALL FINALS
Pinto League—Division A
Alexander Hardware 6, Schlossberg Realty, 0
HRs: Fingerhut, Kalicki,
J. Chen, N. Chen, Di Poppo
(Winning pitcher: Fingerhut)

Forecast for June

Sagittarius (Nov. 21 to Dec. 20)

You're finally in the winner's circle. Fame and fortune could be yours. People are starting to take you seriously. New friends surround you.

Summer Weather Forecast

Meteorologist Vince Jerome, from WMTO, predicts an unusually dry summer with mild temperatures for most of Missouri.

A Final Message from Howard J. Fingerhut

Many authors of how-to books write very long Final Messages. I am unable to do that. I'm leaving tomorrow for Redbird Sports Camp, so I have to pack my trunk. I also need to make photocopies of my book for Allyson and Mrs. Muckley to take to New York.

I reread my book for a *fourth* time while I was numbering the pages. I think I kept most of the promises I made in my Personal Message. Many of my chapters were short, and I remembered to use subtitles.

I also think I taught you (1) how to start your business; (2) how to keep it running; and (3) how to make a very big profit.

I have no way of knowing, at this time, how much my book has changed your life. I do know it has certainly changed mine. Last September I had no plans whatsoever to bunk with Spenser at Redbird this summer. I also had no plans to hire and write to Allyson during camp. Oh, and to mention her name in my how-to book and diary.

As Mrs. Muckley says, "For goodness' shakes!"

Amber, it seems, likes to hide in locked bathroom stalls, and she told everyone I will never be important. She said a writer is not an author until he sells the book he wrote. Allyson and I told her, "It's just a matter of time."

I hope you enjoyed my book. To thank all of my readers, I hired Monica to print the coupon below. Please use it toward the purchase of my next book. I don't know yet what the subject will be. Maybe sports, since I'll be away at camp.

Have a nice summer!
Howie

P.S. Ms. Robedeaux accepted my book for extra credit!